STERLING and the distinctive Sterling logo are
registered trademarks of Sterling Publishing Co., Inc.

Library of Congress Cataloging-in-Publication Data

Le Gall, Pierre.
  [Constance en pension. English]
  Constance and the Great Escape / by Pierre Le Gall and Éric Héliot ;
[translation by Shannon Rowan and Robert Agis].
     p. cm.
  Originally published: Constance en pension. France : Hachette Livre, 2007.
  Summary: Constance's parents and teachers decide that she needs to be
  sent to a strict boarding school but Constance, determined to reunite
with her beloved cat, Tiny, devises a plan to return home.
  ISBN 978-1-4027-6649-7
  [1. Boarding schools--Fiction. 2. Schools--Fiction. 3. Behavior--Fiction.
4. Parent and child--Fiction.] I. Héliot, Éric. II. Rowan, Shannon.
III. Agis, Robert. IV. Title.
  PZ7.L4537Con 2009
  [E]--dc22   2008046856

10 9 8 7 6 5 4 3 2 1

Originally published in France under the title Constance en pension
© 2007 Hachette Livre
English translation by Shannon Rowan and Robert Agis.
English translation copyright © 2009 Sterling Publishing Co., Inc.

Published in 2009 by Sterling Publishing Co., Inc.
387 Park Avenue South, New York, NY 10016
Distributed in Canada by Sterling Publishing
c/o Canadian Manda Group, 165 Dufferin Street
Toronto, Ontario, Canada M6K 3H6
Distributed in the United Kingdom by GMC Distribution Services
Castle Place, 166 High Street, Lewes, East Sussex, England BN7 1XU
Distributed in Australia by Capricorn Link (Australia) Pty. Ltd.
P.O. Box 704, Windsor, NSW 2756, Australia

Printed in China in January 2009

Sterling ISBN 978-1-4027-6649-7

For information about custom editions, special sales, premium and
corporate purchases, please contact Sterling Special Sales Department
at 800-805-5489 or specialsales@sterlingpublishing.com.

CONSTANCE
and the
Great Escape

by Pierre Le Gall
illustrated by Éric Héliot

STERLING

New York / London

My name is Constance.
My only friend in the world is Tiny,
my adorable little cat.

My parents don't want
Tiny and me to be happy.
They are completely unfair.

My teachers at school
are just as bad.

Then one day my parents and
the school principal plotted
to make my life truly miserable.

They found a new punishment:
they were sending me to *prison*.

I couldn't believe my ears!
"It's for your own good,"
lied my cruel parents.

"Welcome to the Jolly Boarding School.
I am Ms. Joy, the headmistress."

"You will learn respect and discipline,
my dear. You'll like it here—I promise."

"If all goes well, you will go home one weekend each month. Now a classmate will show you to your room."

"Hi. I'm Lily the Terror...
at least that's who I was before
my parents left me here."

"Now I am just plain Lily."
And poor Lily took out a big
handkerchief and started to cry.

Very quickly, I realized that this place was *not* for my own good. My parents were just trying to separate me from my adorable little cat.

Poor little Tiny, all alone in
that evil house. I had to escape
from this trap, and fast!

At midnight, I came up with
the perfect plan. I would *pretend*
to be the ideal inmate.

"I love waking up early enough
to see the sun come up!"

"What a tasty breakfast.
I'm ready for a great day of classes."

"We are here to learn
and get smart."

"Everyone is so nice here.
You know just what is
best for us, Ms. Joy."

"Oh, yes!
I would like to stay here forever!
The discipline is great!"

"Miss Constance,
I have asked your parents
to come today."

"You have wasted my time!
This is not the place for your child.
We are busy with *difficult* children here."

"Perhaps you should try
being nicer to your little girl.
Good-bye."

"Now *that's* a child who seems
to be on the right path."

No one can separate me from Tiny,
my adorable little cat!